The Roads That Raised Me

OrangeBooks Publication

1st Floor, Rajhans Arcade, Mall Road, Kohka, Bhilai, Chhattisgarh 490020
Website: **www.orangebooks.in**

First Edition, 2025

ISBN: 978-93-7426-865-0

Price: Rs. 199.00

Printed in India

THE ROADS THAT RAISED ME

RISHI RAMESH GOLAIT

OrangeBooks Publication
www.orangebooks.in

Dedication

For Aai and Baba, who taught me how to stand still in the rain.

Acknowledgements

Every story is built not just on words, but on people, those who stood beside you when life felt uncertain, who believed in you when you doubted yourself, and who quietly shaped the person you became.

To my parents: Aai and Baba, your strength, simplicity, and faith are the roots of everything I am. Every value I hold, every decision I take, carries a piece of your teaching. Even though you are not here, I still feel your presence in every step I take.

To my sister: Your calm, courage, and belief have been my anchor through every storm. You reminded me that family is not defined by distance or time, but by the love that never fades.

To my Brother-in-law: Thank you for being a part of our family; it truly means more than words can express. Thank you for accepting my sister with an open heart and giving her the space to share her journey alongside yours. In so many quiet, unspoken ways, your guidance and presence have supported me, shaped me, and helped me see life with greater patience and understanding. I know this bond and your influence will stay with me always.

To my wife: You are my peace, my reason, and the voice that turned silence into purpose. You taught me that love does not need to be loud to be real. Thank you for walking this bridge with me, patiently, fearlessly, and always with hope.

To my close friends, especially those who never stopped checking in, encouraging me, and believing that my story was worth telling, thank you. Your presence made the difficult roads easier to cross.

A special thank you to ***Dr. Ketaki Chavan Pawar (Author of The Emotional Reset)*** whose words on emotional healing and acceptance guided me through some of my darkest chapters. You reminded me that peace begins within, not around.

And to everyone who shared ***a chai, a conversation,*** or a moment of kindness knowingly or unknowingly, you became a part of this story.

Lastly, to the readers, if these pages make you pause, reflect, or smile even once, then this journey was worth it. Because life isn't about where we end up, it's about the roads, the people, and the moments that raise us along the way.

Tables of Contents

Chapter – 1
The Place That Raised Me

"The place that raised you isn't your destination; it is your beginning."

A place somewhere in India raised a child with many hopes and emotions. A place (Indore) where mornings smelled of burnt wood and tea leaves, and evenings sounded like old radio songs drifting through half-open windows. It wasn't a small town on the map, but it felt small in dreams. Everyone knew everyone, and everything seemed already decided long before you arrived in it. You didn't choose what you would become; you simply followed the path that had been cleared before you.

Our house stood at the edge of a narrow lane, painted a dull yellow that caught sunlight just enough to look warm. The walls were thin, you could hear the neighbours discussing onion prices or cricket scores as if their words could travel through plaster. It was not grand, but it was a home small enough that my mother could call from the kitchen and I would hear her even if I was pretending to study.

Every morning started with the whistle of the pressure cooker, the hum of a ceiling fan fighting the heat, and my father's voice reminding me to get ready for school before eight. My mother would hand me a tiffin box, always warm and smelling faintly of ghee. We lived by rhythm: breakfast at 07:30 am, my father's scooter leaving by 08:15 am, the same newspaper folded in half on the table, and the same quiet between my parents that filled the house like invisible smoke.

The walk to school was my favourite part of the day. I would meet my friends at the corner, Chinmay, Jigar, who always forgot his geometry box, and Nitin, whose bag carried more snacks than books. We would stop at the same chai stall where the old man with betel, stained teeth played Kishore Kumar songs on a dusty radio. He would wink and pour us tiny cups of overly sweet tea, pretending not to see the uniforms that betrayed our truancy.

By the time we reached school, the sun had already started burning through our white shirts. The assembly ground smelled of chalk dust, sweat, and ambition. Teachers stood in lines like guards at a parade, and we, their soldiers, repeated the same pledges every morning to obey, to work hard, to become someone. I didn't know what ***"someone"*** meant back then, only that it sounded important and unreachable.

I was never the teacher's favourite. Not brilliant, not troublesome, just one of the boys who sat in the middle rows and kept his head low. But out on the ground, I came alive. Cricket, football, running, it didn't matter what game it was; I could lose myself in motion. I wasn't the biggest or strongest, but I was fast and sharp. The kind of kid who didn't need encouragement, just a chance.

That chance rarely came.

In my house, sports were a waste of time.

"गेम पेट नहीं भरते," बाबा हमेशा कहा करते थे, "किताबें भरती हैं।"

He was a banker, disciplined, methodical, believing in things that could be counted. For him, success was a number. For me, it was the feeling of the wind in my hair as I ran barefoot across the field. We were never wrong, just different.

Once, during the annual sports day, our PT teacher asked me to fill in for another student who had fallen sick. I ran like the ground itself was pushing me forward and came second, close enough to taste victory. The applause was brief, but for a moment I believed the world had noticed me. That evening, I told my father, expecting something more than a nod.

“Good,” he said, without looking up from his newspaper. ***“Now focus on studies.”***

I remember that silence more than any applause.

After school, I would drop my bag at home and rush to the old ground near the post office, a patch of uneven earth with one rusted goalpost and trees that marked our boundaries. That place was my freedom. The world outside those lines didn’t matter not the marks, not the lectures, not the invisible weight of expectations. The sky would blush pink as the sun dipped, and the smell of frying pakoras drifted through the air. We would play until the streetlights flickered on like gentle reminders that childhood had curfews.

Sometimes I would return home with scraped knees. My mother would sigh, wipe the wounds with Dettol, and whisper, "Your father will scold you if he sees." But she would still smile, as if secretly proud that I wasn't as mechanical as him.

I never said it, but she was the quiet hero of our home, a woman who held peace together like fragile glass, knowing any wrong word could make it shatter.

Evenings were the hardest. My father came home tired, his shirt damp from the day's heat, his temper wrapped in silence. My mother would serve dinner while avoiding his eyes. Some nights, their voices would rise not shouting, but sharp enough to cut the calm. I would sit in the corner, pretending to read, listening to every word I wasn't supposed to hear.

They fought about small things, money, family visits, or how I spent too much time outside. But underneath it all was something larger: the weight of lives that had drifted apart while still sharing the same table.

When you grow up in a house full of unspoken things, you learn to stay quiet. You learn that silence can be safer than the truth.

Love existed, I could feel it, but it was buried under the burden of pride, duty, and fear of being misunderstood.

I needed words, guidance, a hand on my shoulder. Instead, I found silence.

As the years passed, I studied harder partly out of discipline, partly to keep the peace. I told myself this was how life worked: people traded dreams for security and called it responsibility. I still played whenever I could, though less often, and only when no one was watching.

Then, one monsoon evening, my father announced that he had been transferred to Mumbai. He said it casually over dinner, between two spoonfuls of dal. “It’s a good opportunity,” he said. “A bigger branch. Better future.”

I nodded, not because I understood, but because I had learned to agree.

We packed our lives into cardboard boxes, old utensils, books, photo frames, and a few broken trophies. On the last day, I went to our ground one final time. The field was empty, the mud still damp from rain. I stood there, barefoot, letting the soil cling to my feet like it didn't want me to leave. It felt strange leaving behind something that had never really belonged to me, yet defined me.

The train to Mumbai left early morning. I remember sitting by the window, watching Indore shrink, the station, the roofs, the skyline that once felt like the whole world. My mother kept adjusting the luggage, my father kept checking tickets, and I kept looking out, wondering if peace had to be so heavy to carry.

Outside, the fields rolled past like memories I wasn't ready to forget. Inside, the silence between my parents returned familiar, uninvited, constant.

Mumbai was our hometown, my father said. But for me, it was a city of strangers.

It promised bigger roads, brighter lights, and endless noise, everything Indore never had. Yet, deep inside, I already missed the quiet lanes, the familiar faces, the evenings that smelled of dust and pakoras. Indore had given me innocence. Mumbai, I knew, would give me awareness.

Sometimes, I still think about those days, the boy who ran faster than his future, who played without purpose, who believed every evening could end in laughter. That boy didn't know yet that peace can hide storms, that love can exist behind walls, that silence can grow louder than words.

But he was learning. Slowly. Clumsily. Quietly.

When the train pulled into Mumbai Central, my father looked at me and said, "This is where life begins."

Maybe he was right. Maybe it did.

But as I stepped onto the platform, I couldn't shake the feeling that something had stayed behind in Indore, something I would spend years trying to find again.

The places that raised me never really left. They still live inside me in my voice when I stay silent, in my choices when I hesitate, and in my heart when I long for peace.

That morning, as I followed my father through the crowd, I didn't know it yet, but the boy from Indore was about to meet the man he would one day become.

Chapter – 2
The Weight of Choices

"Families are like branches on a tree — we grow in different directions, yet our roots remain one."

Mumbai — The City That Did Not Ask Who I Was

When we reached Mumbai, it did not feel like a city.

It felt like a living thing breathing loudly, impatiently, endlessly.

The moment we stepped out, everything moved at once. Horns overlapped like arguments that never ended. People walked fast, not looking at faces, only at directions. The air felt heavier, not just with pollution, but with urgency as if the city itself was running late and did not care who it left behind.

My father looked comfortable there.

"This is home," he said, almost proudly.

I looked around and wondered how noise could be called home.

For me, Mumbai felt like chaos wearing the mask of opportunity. Everyone said dreams lived here, but no one talked about how tired those dreams looked. The city did not pause. It did not welcome. It only absorbed.

We moved into a modest two-bedroom flat in a crowded housing society. The kind where privacy was a luxury and silence was rare. You could hear every neighbour's television through thin walls, smell their cooking before you even opened your windows, and learn their routines without ever speaking to them.

Life was shared walls, sounds, and frustrations.

My mother unpacked slowly, her movements careful. She was expecting a child then, carrying life while adjusting to a city that barely noticed her. Between half-open cartons and folded clothes, there was a quiet hope in her eyes, a belief that maybe this move would bring something gentler with it.

A few months later, my sister was born.

She was small, pink-faced, and fragile, like she had arrived too softly for a city this loud. I remember holding her for the first time. Her fingers wrapped around mine instinctively, as if she already trusted me, as if she knew I would always be there.

That moment did something to our home.

Even my father softened for a while. His voice lowered. His steps slowed. For a few days, laughter returned, hesitant but real. The house sounded lighter, as if her cries had pushed away the silence that lived between my parents. It felt like joy had found a way in through the cracks.

But Mumbai does not let moments linger.

Soon, the pace returned. Work schedules hardened. Conversations shortened. The city reminded us gently, then firmly, that tenderness had deadlines.

Relatives who had existed only in phone calls and faded stories suddenly became real people with opinions. Uncles patted my head and told me I had grown tall, as if height were an achievement. Aunts smiled warmly while measuring me against their sons, their comparisons wrapped in affection but sharp enough to leave marks.

Back then, there were no video calls. Only imagination stretched across distance. Meeting them felt like meeting characters from a story I had half-forgotten. Everyone asked the same question—

"What will you become when you grow up?"

I smiled every time.

Because I didn't know.

And because no one really wanted an honest answer.

School began again, new uniform, unfamiliar classrooms, faces that didn't know my past. At first, I felt invisible. Then slowly, I found a few friends. We bonded over shared tiffins, cricket cards traded secretly, and punishments we served together for reasons none of us remembered later.

I was above average in studies. The kind who passed without panic, who understood enough to survive but never enough to shine. Teachers never worried about me, and no one celebrated me either.

What truly made me feel alive was sports.

The ground became my escape, cricket, football, running, anything that let me forget the weight of expectations waiting at home. On the field, mistakes were allowed. You fell, you got up, you tried again. No comparisons. No marks. Just movement.

That rhythm made sense to me.

But it didn't make sense to my father.

***

Science — A Decision Made Without Me

In my father's world, everything came down to marks.

Marks were proof. Marks were safe. Marks were respected.

Every family gathering felt like a performance review. Someone's son cracked Engineering. Someone joined the Merchant Navy. Someone got into MBBS. Their stories floated around the room like reminders, quiet but relentless, that success had a narrow definition.

When my 10th results came, my father didn't ask me what I wanted.

He decided.

"You will take Science."

There was no discussion. No pause. No curiosity. Just certainty.

I nodded not because I agreed, but because nodding had become my safest response. In our house, nodding meant peace. Questions meant conflict. And at that age, peace felt more important than honesty.

So I joined Science, because that's what sons do.

They continue the dreams their fathers never finished.

But Chemistry wasn't made for me. Neither was Physics. The formulas felt like a foreign language spoken too fast. Numbers danced on the page without meaning, and every failure made the room feel smaller.

I tried. I really did. Late nights, forced concentration, silent prayers before exams. But nothing stayed, not because I was careless, but because my heart was not there.

Pressure stayed instead.

One day, after gathering courage for weeks, I told my father I wanted to change to a B.Sc. I even had a reputed college ready to take me. I thought maybe now he would understand.

He did not.

"That's a waste," he said.

"You will end up repairing computers in some shop. Is that the life you want?"

His words weren't cruel. They were born from fear, from wanting me to be safe, respected, secure. But fear spoken without listening still wounds.

I didn't argue. I couldn't. He was the only earning member. In our home, his word wasn't just authority, it was survival.

If I resisted, his voice rose. Not just at me, but at everything I represented: youth, resistance, possibility. My mother stayed quiet, her eyes pleading for peace more than justice.

So we compromised.

Not on my dreams, but on agreement.

I took up a diploma course. Not because I wanted to, but because it was the only path left that didn't lead to war at home. Machines and circuits never spoke to me the way words or open grounds once did. Classes felt lifeless. Learning felt mechanical.

I finished the course with relief, not pride.

By then, I had learned something no syllabus teaches you: that in some homes, survival is often mistaken for success.

***

The Diploma Years — Learning Without Belonging

The diploma years passed slowly, like days measured only by attendance and deadlines.

The classrooms were filled with machines, wires, diagrams, and instructors who spoke with certainty about things I never felt connected to. They explained circuits as if they were living truths, but to me, they were just lines on paper, cold, precise, indifferent.

I attended classes. I completed assignments. I passed exams.

But nothing stayed with me.

Not because I was lazy, but because my heart had already learned to switch itself off. Somewhere between choosing Science without choice and landing in a diploma course without desire, I had stopped expecting learning to feel alive.

I watched other students around me, some genuinely interested, some pretending better than I could. They spoke about future jobs, factories, and promotions. I nodded along, just like I had learned to do at home.

At night, I sometimes wondered what I would have been good at if someone had asked me early enough. Writing, maybe. Sports, definitely. Or something I had not even discovered yet.

But wondering did not change anything.

At home, the routine stayed the same. My father believed I was on the right track now. My mother watched quietly, sensing what I never said. And my sister grew laughing, learning, unaware of the quiet bargains being made around her.

When I finally completed the diploma, there was no celebration. Just relief.

Relief that it was over.

Relief that I did not have to pretend anymore.

But relief did not come with direction.

***

Looking for Work — When Rejection Becomes Routine

Finding a job after the diploma was not easy.

For diploma holders, opportunities were limited, salaries were low, and expectations were strangely high. Every interview felt like a test not just of skills, but of confidence I did not fully have.

"Why should we hire you?"

"Where do you see yourself in five years?"

I answered politely, honestly, and without conviction. Because how do you sell a future you do not believe in?

Rejections came quietly. Some through emails. Some through silence. Some through promises that never turned into calls. At first, each rejection hurt sharply. Then, slowly, they began to blend into each other.

My father grew restless.

"You have to start earning," he said.

"It's time you take responsibility."

Maybe he was right. Maybe responsibility should have come earlier. But I was only twenty-one. I still wanted to learn, to explore, to try something that felt like mine.

Instead, I failed again.

Not loudly.

Not visibly.

But in a way that eats at you slowly.

The kind of failure that does not show on certificates, but settles into your posture, your silence, your sleep.

***

The BPO — A Compromise with a Headset

After months of trying, I took a job in a BPO.

It was not a dream.

It was a compromise to wear a headset.

The first day felt strange. Bright lights, glass walls, ID cards, and people who spoke confidently into microphones as if their voices were armour. I was assigned night shifts. My world flipped overnight. Days became sleep, nights became survival.

The calls were endless.

Angry customers. Confused customers. Customers who treated you like a mistake they hadn't ordered. I learned to smile with my voice, to apologise for things I had not done, to stay calm while being blamed for everything.

At first, it drained me.

But slowly, something unexpected happened.

I found people.

People who laughed despite exhaustion. Who shared tiffins at 2 a.m. Who spoke openly about EMIs, family pressure, broken relationships, and postponed dreams. We came from different cities, languages, and backgrounds, but inside that office, we were equal, equally tired, equally hopeful.

They became my chosen family.

We celebrated small wins: first salary, first promotion, first month without errors. We complained together, supported each other, and learned that life was not easy for anyone.

Outside, the world judged us by job titles and pay slips. Inside, we were just trying to survive.

***

Ten Years — When Time Moves Quietly

I stayed there for almost ten years.

Ten years of night shifts.

Ten years of fake smiles and vending-machine coffee.

Ten years of watching others move ahead while I stayed still.

Some people left. Some grew. Some found clarity. I stayed not because I loved the work, but because stability felt safer than uncertainty.

During those years, I felt my childhood dreams blur the boy in Indore chasing a ball across an open ground, believing effort alone was enough. Life had taught me otherwise.

Yet, I never stopped moving.

My mother's words stayed with me, like a small light I refused to let go of:

"No matter how difficult your road is, always keep moving. You will have a bright future."

I did not argue.

I did not question.

I just kept walking, one paycheck at a time.

***

The People Who Made the Nights Bearable

There was one colleague, maybe more than one, but one stands out even now.

We did not become friends instantly. Friendship in night shifts happens slowly, between shared yawns and half-finished sentences. We started with casual nods near the coffee machine, then short complaints about calls that never ended, and finally long conversations during breaks when sleep refused to come.

We talked about everything except ambition.

Because ambition felt like a luxury.

He spoke about his father's illness, how every salary slip was already spent before it reached his hand. Someone else talked about a marriage postponed year after year. Another joked about promotions as if they were myths told to keep people hopeful.

Listening to them, I realised something quietly unsettling

I was not alone in my confusion.

Everyone there was carrying something heavy, invisible to the outside world. We learned to laugh through it. Dark humour became survival. At 3 a.m., exhaustion makes honesty easier. We spoke openly in those hours about fear, regret, and the lives we thought we would live by now.

Those conversations saved me more than any motivational speech ever could.

Because for the first time, I was not being compared.

I was being understood.

***

The Night I Almost Walked Away

There was one night I remember clearly.

The call had gone badly. The customer shouted, insulted, and blamed. I followed the script, apologised, and stayed calm. When the call ended, I removed my headset slowly and stared at the desk in front of me.

Something inside me felt empty.

Not angry.

Not sad.

Just tired.

Tired of pretending.

Tired of being polite under pressure.

Tired of living a life that felt paused.

I walked out during my break and stood near the building's exit. The city was quiet in a way it never was during the day. The road lights flickered. A stray dog slept near the gate. For a moment, I thought, *What if I just do not go back in?*

No resignation.

No backup plan.

Just leaving.

But then reality returned gently, cruelly.

Rent.

Family expectations.

My mother's silent faith.

I went back inside.

Not because I was brave, but because walking away without direction felt scarier than staying.

That night taught me something important:

Sometimes strength is not about making bold exits. Sometimes it's about staying long enough to understand yourself.

***

Becoming Someone, I Did not Recognise

Years passed quietly after that.

Promotions came slowly. Responsibilities increased. I trained new employees—people younger than me, hungrier than me. Some stayed. Some left quickly, already chasing something better.

I noticed myself changing.

I spoke less.

Observed more.

Stopped explaining my choices to people who never tried to understand.

At family gatherings, the questions continued, but I had learned how to answer without answering. A smile here. A vague response there. Inside, I carried a growing awareness, life had shaped me, whether I had agreed to it or not.

I was not the boy who arrived in Mumbai anymore.

But I was not sure who I had become either.

And maybe that's what adulthood really is, not becoming who you dreamed of, but slowly understanding who you are.

***

The Quiet Realisation

One evening, while returning home after a long shift, I watched the city wake up as I prepared to sleep. Vendors are setting up stalls. Children waiting for school buses. Office-goers rushing with purpose.

Life was moving forward.

And so was I just not loud.

That's when it struck me:

I had not failed the way I once believed.

I had survived.

I had learned patience.

Endurance.

Empathy.

I had learned that dignity does not come from titles, and worth is not decided by comparison charts. It comes from continuing even when the road feels borrowed.

Those years did not give me clarity.

But they gave me resilience.

And sometimes, resilience is the foundation that clarity stands on.

Chapter – 3
The Quiet That Stayed

"Rock bottom became the solid foundation on which I rebuilt my life."

That night, I was returning home from my usual night shift.

Mumbai was half-asleep, but never fully at rest. Streetlights flickered like tired eyes struggling to stay open. Stray dogs chased shadows for reasons only they understood. The air was thick, heavy with the smell of early rain and wet roads, as if the city itself was holding its breath.

As the auto moved through familiar lanes, I felt something strange in my chest. Not fear exactly something quieter. A discomfort that had no shape or name. The kind of feeling you try to ignore because acknowledging it feels foolish. I told myself I was just tired. Night shifts do that to you. They blur thoughts, make emotions heavier than they need to be.

Still, that feeling followed me all the way home.

I unlocked the door slowly and stepped inside. The house was unusually still. Too still. Normally, even silence had a rhythm: my mother moving in the kitchen, the sound of a vessel being placed back on the shelf, the faint hum of the television from my father's room. That night, there was nothing.

My mother was resting, or so I assumed. My father was in his room. My sister had gone away for her studies, so it was just the three of us. I did not check on anyone. I did not ask questions. I wish I had.

I changed my clothes and lay down, telling myself I would sleep for a few hours. My body was exhausted, but my mind refused to settle. That strange feeling returned again and again, circling like a warning I couldn't decode. I turned sides, closed my eyes, and opened them again. Somewhere deep inside, something kept whispering that this night mattered.

Around ten in the morning, everything shattered.

My father's voice cut through the house loud, panicked, and cracked in a way I had never heard before.

"Son! Get up! Something happened to Mom!"

I jumped out of bed, my heart pounding before my feet touched the floor. My body moved faster than my thoughts. When I ran into the room, she was lying there still, her eyes closed, her breathing shallow, uneven.

I held her immediately, calling her name again and again. My voice sounded unfamiliar, distant, like it belonged to someone else. Her body felt lighter than it should have, fragile in a way that terrified me.

She took three breaths.

Heavy. Uneven. Final.

The kind of breaths that do not ask for help.

The kind that sounds more like goodbyes than gasps.

And then… nothing.

She was gone.

Right there.

Under my arms.

I do not remember how long I sat frozen. Time stopped behaving normally. Seconds felt endless. Minutes disappeared completely. The world went silent as if someone had switched everything off at once.

Inside me, something broke without sound.

We still rushed to the hospital. Hope is strange like that, it survives even when truth is standing right in front of you. The drive felt unreal. Roads I had travelled hundreds of times looked unfamiliar. The hospital smelled sharp, sterile, cruelly alive.

Doctors checked. Wrote a few things down. Avoided eye contact.

Then they said the words no one is ever prepared for.

“She’s gone.”

That was it.

No explanation.

No warning.

No second chance.

Everything stopped.

Time.

Breath.

Noise.

The house we returned to no longer felt like a house. It felt hollow. As if her absence had changed the structure of the walls themselves. Her voice, once so constant, so gentle, was suddenly nowhere. Even the walls looked different, like they were holding back tears they didn't know how to release.

Relatives arrived one after another. Faces blurred. Voices overlapped. Condolences were offered softly, carefully, like fragile gifts no one knew where to place. Everyone said the same thing.

"Be strong."

No one said how.

No one knew what had happened. She had not been unwell. There were no signs, no warnings, no long hospital stories. She just left. Quietly. Like she had lived without disturbing anyone.

My sister came the next day. Her face was pale, swollen with tears she hadn't had time to release properly. She held me tightly, both of us shaking, trying not to fall apart in front of others. In that embrace, we were no longer adults—we were children who had lost the one place that felt safe.

She stayed until the cremation. Then she had to return for her final exams.

I did not stop her.

I knew studies mattered.

I knew Mom would have wanted that.

But when she left that night, the house felt emptier than ever. I realised then that grief has its own kind of silence. One that does not end when people leave. One that settles into the corners of rooms and refuses to move.

After that, I tried to keep things together.

I went back to work.

I came home.

I followed routines.

But nothing felt the same.

My father's shouting returned sharper, louder, more frequent. Maybe anger was the only language he had left. Maybe grief had nowhere else to go. I did not argue. I did not respond. I let it pass through me.

My mother's absence made the house colder. Even when I was inside it, it no longer felt like home.

My sister completed her engineering and started preparing for her MBA. She worked hard, just like Mom had always told us to. Then one day, news came that she had been selected at a reputed MBA college in Bangalore.

Everyone was proud.

Even my father smiled. A rare, fragile moment.

The day she left, I helped her pack. Folded clothes. Closed bags. Pretended everything was fine. She hugged me tightly before leaving. I told her, "Don't worry about things here."

But when she walked out the door with her suitcase, something inside me collapsed again.

She was not just leaving for her studies.

She was leaving behind the last piece of warmth in the house.

For the first time in my life, I felt completely alone.

Nights became longer after that. I sat by the window, staring at city lights that no longer comforted me. In a few years, I had gone from a boy chasing a cricket ball in Indore to a man sitting in a room that no longer felt alive.

Sometimes I imagined my mother's voice soft, familiar, asking if I had eaten. Sometimes I heard her humming an old song in my head, and for a moment, I almost believed she was still there.

But she wasn't.

She had taken the peace of our home with her.

I began dreaming of a life that felt different. A home where voices were gentle. Where love was not measured by control or silence. A family built on kindness.

But every time I looked at my father, the anger, the loneliness, the walls around him, I wondered if that kind of life was even possible for me.

I did not hate him.

I just did not understand him.

Maybe he had his own wounds.

Maybe silence was the only way he knew how to love.

But that silence…

It had cost us everything.

Years later, I understood something grief teaches without mercy.

Grief does not end.

It just learns to live quietly inside you.

It becomes part of your breathing.

Part of your pauses.

That's what she left behind.

Not emptiness.

But quiet.

A quiet that stayed.

Chapter – 4
The Comfortable Cage

"And then one day, life reminds you, you never needed walls, only courage to begin again."

When we shifted from Mumbai to Bangalore, it felt like life was giving me another chance.

Not a loud one. Not the kind that arrives with celebration or certainty.

Just a quiet opportunity to start over, the kind that does not announce itself but waits patiently, hoping you notice.

Mumbai had taught me how to endure.

Bangalore, I hoped, might teach me how to breathe again.

After years of silence and heavy mornings, I was finally going to live with my sister again. That thought alone carried a strange comfort. Growing up, she had always been the constant when emotions ran high, when the house felt tense, when words failed. Somewhere along the way, adulthood had scattered us into separate lives, separate cities, separate responsibilities. Living together again felt like reclaiming a piece of myself I had misplaced without realising it.

The moment I saw her at the station, waving with that same familiar smile, something inside me softened. It wasn't dramatic. There were no tears, no tight hugs that lingered too long. Just a quiet warmth spreading through my chest, the kind that tells you you're not alone anymore. It had been too long since our home had laughter, too long since joy had arrived without effort.

We moved into a small flat. Nothing fancy. No big balconies or designer furniture. Just two rooms, a kitchen, and a window that let the city in. Yet the moment we unlocked the door and stepped inside, it felt ours. Not rented. Not temporary. Ours.

For the first time in years, the walls didn't echo sadness.

They echoed us.

Shared jokes that came without thinking. Late - night conversations that wandered without direction. Sibling fights over silly things, who finished the snacks, whose turn it was to cook, and why the playlist always leaned toward her choices.

And then there was the comforting sound of her humming in the kitchen, soft and absent-minded, as if she did not even realise she was doing it.

Every corner of that flat carried warmth. A warmth I hadn't felt since Aai was around.

My sister had always been my calm. She had this rare ability to turn chaos into conversation, to slow things down just enough for emotions to breathe. When my thoughts grew heavy, she didn't try to fix them. She listened. When I spiralled into silence, she filled the space gently—not with advice, but with presence. She reminded me, without ever saying it aloud, that life still had softness left in it.

We cooked together on Sundays, turning ordinary meals into rituals. We argued over music while chopping vegetables, laughed over half-burnt rotis, and sat quietly afterwards, sharing tea without feeling the need to speak. Some evenings, we talked about work—about bad days, good colleagues, small victories. Other nights, we drifted into memories. Childhood incidents. Old festivals. Moments we had forgotten, we remembered.

Sometimes, dreams slipped into our conversations, too. Not bold declarations, just hesitant thoughts. Things we wanted but were still afraid to name fully, as if speaking them aloud might invite disappointment.

Life, for once, felt kind.

I found a decent job in Bangalore. Not glamorous. Not the kind you dream of as a child. But steady. Predictable. The pay was enough to cover expenses and save a little. The colleagues were polite, and the workload was manageable. And the city—it had a pulse that felt young and alive, a rhythm that kept moving whether you joined it or not.

There were moments—standing in traffic under a warm drizzle, watching signals change slowly—when I'd catch myself thinking, *Maybe life isn't that cruel after all.*

The house that once echoed with silence now held laughter, shared meals, and small moments of peace. The aroma of coffee in the evenings, the sound of rain tapping against the balcony grill, the city lights flickering outside—they became my new comforts. They grounded me. They reassured me that I had landed somewhere safe.

But happiness, I've learned, has a strange way of reminding you of what's missing.

Even as things looked fine from the outside, I knew something inside me had gone quiet. Not broken. Not shattered. Just… muted. Like a voice that once spoke freely but had learned to whisper instead.

I had built a life that was respectable and stable. A life that made sense. But it wasn't mine—not entirely. It felt borrowed, like a role I was playing well enough for applause but not well enough to feel fulfilled.

Often, in moments of stillness, I found myself wondering: *What would I have become if I had chosen differently?*

The boy who once wanted to play, to dream, to create—he had grown into a man who worked, ate, and slept by the clock. Somewhere between responsibility and survival, I had forgotten who I wanted to be. Dreams hadn't disappeared; they had simply been postponed so many times that they learned how to stay silent.

People said I was lucky.

Good job. Good city. Good life.

But luck feels different when you know the cost.

And one thing that hadn't changed—not even after Aai was gone—was Baba's anger.

It didn't fade with time; it only changed shape. What was once loud had become sharp. What was once explosive had turned persistent. His irritation had woven itself into our rhythm, like distant thunder that never fully passed. He called often—sometimes to ask about bills, sometimes about work—but somehow, every conversation found its way back to tension. A raised voice. A sigh heavy with disappointment. An unfinished sentence that hung between us long after the call ended.

At first, I tried to explain. I tried to make him understand that the world was different now—that happiness didn't come only from degrees, promotions, or comparisons with others. That fulfilment looked different for different people.

But explaining felt like shouting into the wind.

So I stopped trying.

Eventually, silence became our safest language—the only way to protect what little peace I had built. He would talk. I would listen. He would command. I would agree. And in the pauses between our words lived everything we never said—the hurt, the fear, the longing for approval that never came.

Still, deep inside, I longed for something simple. Someone who could sit beside me and understand the silence instead of trying to fill it. Someone I could talk to without pretending, without rehearsing my answers, without fearing judgment.

I imagined a partner. Not a perfect one. Just someone who could walk beside me through chaos and calm. A home filled with laughter, not rules. A life built on choice, not obligation.

But every time I thought about bringing someone new into my life, I hesitated.

The thought of introducing them to Baba's temper, to the ghosts that still lived in our family, to the anger that never really died—it stopped me cold. I didn't want anyone to see that side of my world. I didn't want love to inherit wounds it never caused.

So, like many other dreams, I folded this one carefully and placed it on the shelf of *maybe someday*.

That's the thing about comfort—it fools you into believing you are safe.

But sometimes, comfort is just a softer name for surrender.

I had everything I thought I needed: a job, a home, a routine. Yet I often felt like a visitor in my own life, moving through days that didn't quite belong to me.

Some nights, after my sister went to sleep, I'd sit by the window of our Bangalore flat and watch the city lights blur in the rain. Roads shimmered. People hurried under umbrellas. Life moved fast, urgent, alive. And I stood still, observing, untouched.

The rain always reminded me of Indore—of simpler days when dreams didn't scare me. Back then, rain meant freedom. Now, it sounded different. Softer. Sadder. As if it understood what it meant to survive instead of live.

It was peaceful.

But empty.

A calm that didn't heal—just hid what hurt.

Comfort had given me everything: stability, security, silence.

Everything, except myself.

Chapter – 5
The Turning Point

"The wound is the place where the Light enters you."

The rain always reminded me of Indore—of simpler days when dreams didn't scare me. Back then, rain meant freedom. Now, it sounded different. Softer. Sadder. As if it understood what it meant to survive instead of live.

It was peaceful.

But empty.

A calm that didn't heal—just hid what hurt.

Comfort had given me everything: stability, security, silence.

Everything, except myself.

Chapter – 5
The Turning Point

"The wound is the place where the Light enters you."

Some realisations do not strike like lightning.

They do not arrive with drama or warning.

They come quietly, almost politely slipping into your life through an ordinary evening, asking nothing, yet changing everything.

That evening, I sat with a close friend in a café near Indiranagar, Bangalore, the kind that smelled of old songs, coffee, and unhurried conversations. Soft music played in the background, old Hindi songs slowed down just enough to feel nostalgic. The air carried the scent of roasted coffee beans, damp earth, and rain that had just passed through the city and decided to linger.

The café was half full. A couple argued softly in one corner. Two college students leaned over a laptop, pretending to study but mostly laughing. Outside, traffic crawled past, horns blaring without purpose, as if even impatience had grown tired.

We were talking about nothing in particular, work, deadlines, and how Bangalore traffic could turn even the calmest person into a philosopher. We laughed about small inconveniences, shared complaints we had shared a hundred times before. It was comfortable, familiar, and easy.

At some point, the conversation slowed. Not abruptly, just naturally, the way it does when both people sense something unspoken hovering between them.

My friend leaned back and looked at me. Not casually. Not the way people look when they are waiting for their turn to speak. He really looked at me, as if trying to read something written beneath my expressions.

Then he said, almost gently,

"Bhai, you have spent your whole life doing what others wanted."

I smiled—half amused, half dismissive.

He did not smile back.

"What do *you* want?"

The question landed softly.

But it landed deep.

I opened my mouth to answer. Habit took over. My mind began assembling safe responses, something responsible, something acceptable, something that wouldn't invite further questions.

But nothing came out.

Because for the first time, I realised I did not know.

The silence stretched between us was not awkward, just honest. He noticed it immediately & smiled, then not teasing, not victorious, but kind. The kind of smile that understands without judging.

"Think about it," he said, stirring his coffee slowly.

"Before life decides for you again."

We finished our drinks after that, talking about lighter things. He paid the bill. We stepped outside. The rain had stopped, leaving the roads shiny and reflective, as if they were holding secrets of their own.

We said goodbye casually, the way we always did.

But that sentence stayed.

It followed me home, riding beside me in the cab, standing with me in the elevator, unlocking the door with me. It echoed softly in the empty flat, settling into corners I had not visited in years.

What did I want?

The question sounded simple. Almost childish. Yet it shook me more than any failure ever had.

That night, I sat by the window, watching the drizzle return quietly, as if it had unfinished business. Drops slid down the glass, one after another, unhurried. Streetlights blurred into soft halos. Somewhere below, a dog barked once and then fell silent.

I realised how much of my life had been spent waiting.

Waiting for approval.

Waiting for peace.

Waiting for permission.

Waiting for something that always seemed to belong to someone else.

Some changes in life do not arrive with noise.

They do not announce themselves.

They walk in quietly, through the spaces people leave behind.

When my sister found love, I saw something in her eyes that I had not seen in years.

Calmness.

Not excitement. Not the nervous rush people mistake for happiness. But a steady calm, the kind that settles into your bones and stays.

His name was ***Aditya.***

The first time I met him, there was nothing dramatic about the moment. No instant judgments. No exaggerated friendliness. Just a firm but unassuming handshake, eyes that met yours without challenge, and a presence that did not need to prove itself.

He was calm. Grounded. Thoughtful with his words. The kind of man who listened fully before responding. Someone who did not make promises easily, but once he did, you knew they would be kept.

He never said no to responsibility and never overlooked small kindnesses. He held doors open without making it a performance. He remembered details without reminding you that he remembered them.

He was the kind of person who did not try to impress the world.

He simply showed up consistently.

And somehow, that said more than words ever could.

I knew it the moment I saw them together. The way my sister spoke around him. The way she paused less and smiled more. The way the silence between them did not feel heavy or awkward, it felt complete.

I had always believed my sister deserved someone steady. Someone who would hold her heart with care and respect. Someone who would not ask her to shrink, to wait, or to explain herself endlessly.

Aditya was exactly that.

The day she got married, the house felt different.

Not empty.

Full.

Full of memories that knew their time had come.

I watched her walk toward a new life. My chest felt heavy, but my heart felt light. I was happy, truly happy, because I knew she was in safe hands.

Still, when she left, something inside me grew quiet.

Her laughter. Her presence. Her small reminders to eat on time. They had filled the house with life. And now, those sounds belonged somewhere else.

That night, I sat in her room for a long time, staring at the walls, the books, the stillness.

I was not sad.

I was simply aware that love, too, has its seasons—one where you hold on, and one where you learn to let go.

Not long after, my job required me to move to Pune.

Another city.

Another rented room.

Another beginning that didn't feel like one.

The days were full, but the nights stretched endlessly. I had everything stability, salary, order, except warmth.

That's when I met ***Dr. Ketaki Chavan Pawar***, my close friend ***Akshay's*** wife.

She spoke in a way that made silence sound useful. She introduced me to manifestation—not as superstition, but as a discipline of thought.

"When you start believing in the possibility of good," she said, "you make room for it."

At first, I smiled politely. But her words stayed with me.

So I began writing not what was missing, but what I wished to see.

Peace.

Gratitude.

Strength.

Slowly, something inside me began to change. Not loudly. Not dramatically. Just a quiet shift like a door opening somewhere within.

I began to notice the small beauties I had ignored for years, the softness of morning light, the comfort of solitude, the taste of tea when it wasn't rushed.

I was learning to breathe again.

Then one evening, a call shattered that calm.

(Sister Called)

"Baba had suffered a cardiac arrest"!

I rushed to Bangalore, whispering to myself that he would be fine because belief was the only thing stronger than fear.

For days, I stayed by his side, praying silently, holding on to faith.

But destiny has its own way of writing goodbyes.

Baba was gone.

I did not cry.

I did not scream.

I stood still and heard his voice in my head, the same old tone, the same words:

"Even if you fall, do not bend.

The world remembers those who stand."

That day, I did not fall.

After the rituals, my sister sat beside me and said softly,

"Maybe it's time you start living for yourself now. It's never too late."

And somehow, I believed her.

Weeks later, on my birthday, life gifted me something far beyond what I could have wished for.

That day, I met a girl with a gentle, charming presence. Her smile felt like an entire world to me, something words could not quite capture, something beyond my imagination. Her name is **Maina** ***(Name Changed).***"

Marriage did not change my life overnight.

It softened it.

There were no fireworks, no sudden sense of arrival, no dramatic feeling that everything had finally fallen into place. What arrived instead was something far more unfamiliar to me: **consistency without tension**.

Maina and I built our days quietly. Mornings began without urgency. Sometimes with conversation, sometimes with silence that did not need interpretation. She had a way of moving through the house that felt intentional but unforced, as if she trusted time instead of fighting it. Watching her made me realise how long I had lived in anticipation, always waiting for something to go wrong.

With her, I stopped waiting.

Marriage, I learned, is not about grand moments. It's about repetition done gently. About waking up next to someone and not needing to explain the weight you are carrying. About sharing tea without discussing plans. About knowing that even ordinary days are being witnessed.

There were evenings when we sat together after long workdays, tired but present. No pressure to perform happiness. No need to prove love through words. Just the comfort of being understood without translation.

She noticed things I did not speak about.

The way my shoulders tightened during phone calls.

The way I paused before making decisions.

The way silence sometimes felt safer to me than honesty.

She never confronted these things head-on. She did not try to fix me. She simply stayed. And in that staying, something inside me began to unlearn fear.

I told her about Baba slowly. Not in one conversation, but in fragments, stories, habits, moments of anger mixed with care. She listened without defending or diagnosing. She did not reduce him to a villain or me to a victim. She allowed complexity to exist.

That mattered.

Because for the first time, I did not feel like my past was something I had to hide in order to be loved.

Marriage did not erase grief.

But it gave grief somewhere to rest.

There were days when memories surfaced without warning, Aai's voice, Baba's discipline, my sister's laughter filling rooms that no longer existed the same way. Earlier, these memories had felt heavy. Now, they felt complete. As if they belonged to a story that had been told fully, even if it had hurt.

Maina had a way of grounding me in the present. Not forcefully, never with advice or urgency, but through small, human gestures. A hand resting on mine while watching nothing in particular. A question asked softly at the right time. A shared smile that said, *I see you.*

In her presence, I began to understand that peace is not the absence of pain.

It's the absence of fear around pain.

We spoke about the future, but not obsessively. There was no rush to plan everything. No pressure to become something impressive. We spoke instead about how we wanted to feel. About kindness. About building a home that felt safe to return to, not just physically, but emotionally.

For the first time, the idea of **"home"** didn't feel temporary.

I began noticing changes in myself.

I laughed more easily.

I slept more deeply.

I spoke more honestly.

The man who once survived by staying quiet slowly learned that his voice did not have to create conflict. That expression did not always lead to punishment. That love could exist without conditions attached.

Marriage did not make me brave overnight.

But it made me **less afraid**.

There were moments, small, unremarkable moments, when I caught myself feeling content without questioning it. No guilt. No suspicion. Just a gentle acceptance that life, for now, was kind.

And perhaps that was the greatest shift of all.

I had spent years believing that peace was something you earned only after enduring enough. That happiness was fragile and temporary. That stability required the sacrifice of self.

Marriage taught me something quieter, yet deeper.

That you do not lose yourself when you choose the right person.

You finally stop protecting yourself from life.

And in that stopping, in that surrender not to fear, but to trust, I found something I had been searching for without knowing how to ask.

Not perfection.

Not certainty.

But **belonging**.

Chapter – 6
The Hidden Roads Within

"Peace comes from within. Do not seek it without."

— Buddha

I searched for my path in life.

Before I go any further, I want to say this — this story is not just about one person.

It's about many.

It's about the quiet struggles of an ordinary man — the kind of man you see every day, who smiles through his tiredness, carries his dreams silently, and keeps walking no matter how heavy life feels.

It's the story of countless people who never speak about what they truly feel, because everyone is too busy proving who they are to the world.

We live in a time where appearances speak louder than emotions, where success is measured in titles, not peace.

But beneath that noise, hearts are fighting small, unseen battles every single day between what they want and what life allows.

This chapter is for all those who keep going, quietly.

***

Peace doesn't arrive with noise.

It comes quietly like morning light slipping through half-open curtains.

For the first time in years, life felt still. Not perfect, not grand, just still.

Bangalore had slowly turned into home — its slow rains, soft mornings, and familiar cafés had become part of my rhythm.

The city didn't rush me; it let me breathe.

Days blended into one another, not in boredom, but in balance.

There was work, love, and a kind of calm that once felt impossible.

But peace has its own way of revealing things — not what's missing outside, but what's waiting inside.

And one evening, sitting on the balcony with a cup of tea, he realised that the person he had become was finally someone his younger self would recognise.

The boy who once followed everyone's path had finally started walking his own.

It began with small things.

Writing again, not about pain this time, but gratitude.

Helping people at work not because it was his job, but because it felt right.

Listening, truly listening without waiting to reply.

That's when he understood: meaning doesn't come from success; it comes from awareness.

It's not about where you reach, but how you walk.

His partner often reminded him of that without saying much.

She had a way of seeing beauty in small things, the way sunlight hit the floor in the morning, the sound of the first rain, the smell of ginger tea.

She would often say, "Happiness isn't found, it's remembered."

And she was right.

In her quiet way, she taught him that peace isn't a place you find, it's something you build inside you, one honest thought at a time.

He started to understand people differently, too.

Everyone is carrying something: a story, a loss, a hope, and yet we meet them like strangers.

But once you begin to see the pain behind someone's silence, you stop judging and start connecting.

Maybe that's what growing up truly means: learning to see beyond yourself.

Sometimes, late at night, he would think about everything that had happened his childhood dreams, the failures, the fights, the losses, and the love that finally arrived.

And he realised that all of it, every turn, every delay, every scar had been leading him here.

All those outer journeys were never really about places.

They were just roads leading him back to himself.

"The longest journey we take is from our mind to our heart."

Now, when he wakes up each morning, he doesn't ask what he needs to achieve.

He asks how he can make today a little kinder to himself, to others, to life itself.

Because one day, everything we chase money, praise, titles will fade.

But what will remain are the small things:

how we spoke to someone when they were low,

how we kept going when no one believed,

and how we treated ourselves when we were tired.

Those are the real roads, the hidden ones.

The ones that run through the heart and never end.

And maybe, after all these years, he's finally learned peace isn't something you reach.

It's something you remember.

"In the end, we all become stories, not the ones written in words, but the ones remembered in hearts."

— Rishi Golait

Chapter – 7
The Roads of Gratitude

There comes a stage in a man's life when he stops running from the truth and begins sitting with it, not because he finally becomes wise but because he becomes tired.

That is what happened with ***Ameya.***

For years, he fought, resisted, complained, questioned, blamed, doubted—and survived. But survival has a strange habit. It keeps you alive, yes, but it slowly empties you from the inside.

And exhaustion, sometimes, is the doorway to understanding.

That was when gratitude entered his life, not dramatically, not like a sudden awakening, but like light entering a room through a crack in the curtain.

He did not even notice it in the beginning.

But one day, he realised he was not carrying the same weight on his chest. He could breathe a little more freely. He didn't know why. He just knew something inside him had softened.

The Morning That Changed Everything

It was a Tuesday morning, ordinary, like the hundreds before it.

The sun was not special. The breeze was not different.

But something in Ameya was.

He woke up, sat at the edge of his bed, and for the first time in years, he didn't grab his phone.

He didn't check missed emails.

He didn't scroll social media.

He didn't replay yesterday's arguments.

He simply sat quietly.

And in that silence, something shifted.

He looked around his room, small, cluttered, imperfect, but it felt less suffocating that day. He stretched his arms, and the first thought that came to him was:

"I am grateful that I can breathe without worrying today."

It was such a simple thought. So ordinary. Yet it felt like a warm cup of tea placed gently in his hands by life itself.

Later that day, as he walked to the nearby tea stall, he noticed something he had never paid attention to before.

The old vendor smiled at him, not because Ameya bought tea every day, but because the vendor had seen him grow over the years, saw him leave for work hurriedly, saw him come back exhausted, saw him lost in thought, and saw him silent.

That day, when the old man handed him the cup, he said,

"Son, you look lighter today."

And he smiled genuinely, not the polite, forced curve he showed people.

He realised something, Life does not always show you blessings, sometimes, it shows you people who reflect your blessings to you.

The Day He Understood What ***Gratitude*** Really Means -

It did not come from a book or a motivational video.

It came from an incident so ordinary that most people would forget it in 5 minutes.

Ameya was in a cab, stuck in traffic. The heat was unbearable. People were shouting on the road. The driver was irritated. But Ameya sat there quietly.

Noticing.

Observing.

Breathing.

On the left side of the road, he saw a young boy balancing 20 water bottles inside a crate, selling them in the scorching sun. The boy walked barefoot, yet his posture was straight. He smiled at customers. He joked with auto drivers. He adjusted the bottles carefully so they would not fall.

His smile was not fake. It was not forced. It was simply acceptance.

At that moment, Ameya felt something inside him melt.

"If he can smile while fighting life every minute," he thought,

"Why cannot I be grateful for a life that has protected me far more than it has punished me?"

He did not buy a bottle that day.

He bought a lesson.

Gratitude is not about having a perfect life.

It is about recognising that your imperfect life still holds beauty.

The Gratitude Exercise That Changed Him

One night, without any plan, Ameya opened a blank page in his journal and wrote:

"5 Things I am Grateful For Today"

He struggled at first.

His mind was too used to listing problems.

But slowly, he wrote:

1. I am grateful for a roof over my head.
2. I am grateful I can earn and support my family.

3. I am grateful my mother still waits to talk to me.

4. I am grateful my failures did not finish me.

5. I am grateful I am still trying.

He closed the book and slept.

That was the first night in years he did not dream of running or failing.

He dreamt of peace.

Manifestation: Becoming the Man He Imagined

Gratitude naturally led him toward a new habit, **Manifestation.**

Not the exaggerated social-media version.

Not "think positive and magic will happen."

But the real kind:

- Visualising the life he wanted
- Replacing fear-driven thoughts with courageous ones
- Speaking to himself kindly

- Dreaming without apologising
- Believing without doubting his worth

For example:

Example 1 — The Workplace Shift

Earlier, every Monday felt like a threat.

But one day, he entered the office thinking:

"Let today be good. Let me handle everything calmly."

And surprisingly, the day was better.

People responded more respectfully.

Meetings went smoothly.

He did not feel overwhelmed.

Life had not changed.

He had.

Example 2 — Handling Financial Pressure

When bills piled up, he did not panic.

He sat, breathed deeply, made a plan, and told himself:

"Money is a storm. It comes and goes. But I remain."

That mindset alone reduced 50% of his anxiety.

Example 3 — Relationships

Instead of expecting perfect understanding from others, he began appreciating small efforts, a short message, a call, or someone asking if he reached home safely.

Slowly, gratitude replaced resentment.

Realisation: Gratitude Doesn't Change Life, It Changes You

One evening, as he sat on the terrace watching the sun melt behind buildings, he whispered to himself:

"Life was never my enemy…

I just did not know how to read it."

Gratitude did not give him miracles.

It gave him understanding.

It did not remove his struggles.

It made him stronger than his struggles.

It did not change who hurt him.

It changed what he expected from others.

It did not promise a perfect tomorrow.

But it gifted him a peaceful today.

And that was enough.

The Roads of Gratitude Become the Roads Ahead

Ameya finally understood:

Every moment he appreciated returned to him with more calmness.

Every thought he corrected returned as clarity.

Every fear he released returned as freedom.

Gratitude was not the ending of his journey; it was the beginning of becoming a better man.

A man who could love again, trust again, dream again & eventually find peace again.

For the first time in years, he felt ready not for the world, but for himself.

Chapter – 8
The Art of Letting Go, the Art of Moving Forward

There comes a time in every life when silence becomes the loudest teacher.

Not the silence of loneliness, but the silence that arrives when you finally stop fighting life and start listening to it.

Ameya reached that silence after years of carrying the weight on his shoulders weight of expectations, guilt, fear, comparison, responsibilities, and the invisible pressure to be everything for everyone. His journey was not extraordinary; it was painfully ordinary. And that's what made the lessons so important. Because ordinary pain is the most universal kind.

When he looked back, he realised that the biggest changes in his life did not come from achievements. They came from acceptance. They came from learning to let go slowly, painfully, but honestly. They came from shifting how he thought, how he interpreted life, and how he responded to the parts of life he could not control.

This chapter is not about his actions. It is about his understanding. It is not about what happened to him. It is about what he learned from everything that happened. It is not about endings. It is about evolving.

And through his evolution comes the heart of this chapter, the lessons that can change anyone's life if they choose to apply them with sincerity.

This is the chapter where Ameya does not narrate the story anymore.

He speaks to the reader.

He speaks to the human inside everyone.

He shares the wisdom he earned the hard way.

And in doing so, he closes the book not with sorrow, not with triumph, but with clarity.

Ameya learned, first and foremost, that **life cannot be controlled**.

We spend so much time trying to fix things that were never broken, trying to heal people who were never ready, trying to force outcomes that were never meant for us. We become tired, hurt, and confused not because life is cruel, but because life operates on its own timeline.

He learned that not everything requires effort.

Some things require patience.

Some things require allowing.

Some things require stepping aside.

There are moments in life when nothing makes sense. But one day, when you look back, everything looks perfectly aligned. Everything looks intentional. Everything looks necessary.

Ameya realised this late, but he realised it deeply. **Life is not happening against you; it is unfolding for you.**

Every delay protected him from something he did not see.

Every failure redirected him to something he needed.

Every heartbreak expanded him emotionally.

Every disappointment built resilience inside him.

Every loss created space for something better to enter.

Letting go, he learned, is the greatest form of wisdom not because it frees others, but because it frees you.

He learned to let go of people who could not love him the way he needed.

He learned to let go of expectations that exhausted him.

He learned to let go of guilt that was not his responsibility.

He learned to let go of dreams that no longer aligned with who he was becoming.

He learned to let go of the old version of himself, the man who carried pain like a badge.

Letting go was not a moment. It was a process. It was a lesson life taught him again and again, until he finally understood it.

One evening, while sitting alone with a cup of tea, he realised something profound:

"The things I have lost were never meant to stay.

The things I have gained were always meant to find me."

This thought softened him.

It made forgiveness easier.

It made acceptance possible.

It made gratitude natural.

He learned that **people will hurt you**, even those you trust. Not because they are evil, but because humans are imperfect. Some will misunderstand you without trying to know you. Some will judge you without seeing your struggle. Some will leave without closure. Some will love you but still fail you. Some will stay but never understand you.

Ameya used to take everything personally. He believed every hurt meant he was not enough. But life taught him that people act from their own wounds, not from your worth.

Forgiveness, he learned, is not about saying what they did was okay.

Forgiveness is saying, *"I refuse to carry this pain any longer."*

He forgave people not because they asked, but because he deserved peace.

He forgave himself because he finally realised that he had always done the best he could with the understanding he had at the time.

One of the hardest battles Ameya fought was with his own thoughts.

He lived years imagining the worst.

He lived years fearing the future.

He lived years blaming himself.

He lived years stuck between overthinking and regret.

But as he grew, he understood a powerful truth:

Your thoughts shape your world long before your actions do.

Positive thinking is not about pretending everything is fine.

It's about choosing thoughts that support your growth rather than destroy it.

He learned to replace:

"I can't handle this" with "I will find a way."

"I am not enough" with "I am learning."

"Everything is going wrong" with "Something is shifting for me."

"I am failing" with "I am growing."

"I am alone" with "I am becoming stronger."

Slowly, these shifts planted seeds in his mind, and the seeds grew into courage. Courage grew into clarity. Clarity grew into action. Action grew into change. Change grew into peace.

Thinking positively did not remove all his problems. But it removed the unnecessary suffering he added on top of them. He learned that pain is real, but suffering is often created in the mind. Some nights he cried. Some mornings, he felt lost again.

Healing was never a straight line. But every time he felt broken, he came back stronger, not because life became easier, but because he became wise enough to face it without collapsing. He realised that he did not need a perfect life to be happy. He just needed a peaceful heart.

And a peaceful heart is built through three practices:

1. Gratitude
2. Letting go
3. Choosing better thoughts every day

Gratitude became his anchor.

He began noticing small blessings: the comfort of his home, the warmth of his mother's voice, the unexpected kindness of strangers, the resilience he did not know he had. Gratitude made him realise how much goodness existed even in the most mundane days. Letting go became his freedom. He stopped carrying things longer than necessary. He stopped replaying old arguments. He stopped punishing himself for mistakes.

He stopped chasing closure from people who could not give it. And choosing better thoughts became his transformation. He rewired his inner dialogue. He changed how he spoke to himself. He built a healthier relationship with his mind.

One day, he wrote in his journal:

"My life did not change when I healed.

My life changed when I stopped hurting myself with old thoughts."

He learned, slowly but deeply, that he was not defined by:

the mistakes he made,

the failures he faced,

the people he lost,

the fear he lived with,

the dreams he paused.

He was defined by his willingness to begin again.

He understood that beginnings are not grand moments. Beginnings are quiet decisions.

Beginnings are made in the mind long before they appear in the world. He learned that not every ending is a tragedy. Some endings are the universe's way of redirecting you. Some endings are beginnings disguised as pain. He learned that healing does not always come from answers. Sometimes healing comes from peace with unanswered questions.

He learned that real strength is not loud. Real strength is gentle. Real strength is patience.

Real strength is forgiving. Real strength is choosing not to break even when life has every opportunity to shatter you. He learned that life is not about rushing. Life is about rhythm. Life is about flow. Life is about presence.

He learned that peace is not something you find. Peace is something you create. Peace is something you protect. Peace is something you return to.

And finally, he learned that the universe has its own language. A language made of timing, energy, alignment, intention, and purpose.

You may not understand it today. You may not understand it tomorrow.

But one day, when you look back, everything that confused you will make sense.

The people who left, the opportunities that didn't work, the relationships that broke, the plans that failed, the dreams that changed, the fears that held you, the loneliness that taught you, the delays that protected you, the choices that shaped you.

They will all form a picture, a picture of a life that was not perfect, but purposeful.

Ameya realised something profound:

Life is always teaching you who you are becoming.

Every chapter, Every moment, Every breath, Every heartbreak, Every victory, Every silence. It all adds up.

And when he finally stood at the end of this book, this journey, he did not feel victorious.

He felt grateful.

Grateful for the roads that broke him.

Grateful for the roads that healed him.

Grateful for the roads that raised him.

He understood, at last, that life does not want perfection from you.

Life wants presence, Life wants honesty, Life wants acceptance, Life wants effort without attachment, Life wants faith without forcing. Life wants you to let go of what is not yours so it can give you what has always been meant for you.

And with that understanding, Ameya finally stepped forward. Not with fear, not with confusion, but with trust.

This is not the end of his story.

This is the beginning of a new man, A man who walks lightly, A man who thinks wisely, A man who forgives easily, A man who loves deeply, A man who chooses peace over chaos.

A man who has learned the art of letting go.

And as he walks ahead, he carries one truth with him:

You are never lost. You are always becoming who you are.

Epilogue
A Whisper to the Universe

There comes a moment rare, sacred, indescribable when a person finally understands why they had to walk through every fire, every silence, every heartbreak, every lonely night.

Ameya reached that moment.

Not with noise.

Not with celebration.

But with a quiet exhale that felt like the first breath of his life.

He looked at the sky one evening, not searching for answers, but offering his truth.

It was not a prayer.

It was not a wish.

It was not a complaint.

It was an **announcement**.

To life.

To time.

To destiny.

To the universe that watched him crawl, fall, rise, break, rebuild, shatter, and shine again.

He whispered, not loudly, but with a conviction that echoed beyond sound:

"I have arrived.

Not at a destination—

but at myself."

In that moment, everything he had endured aligned like stars forming a constellation.

A pattern he could finally see.

A meaning he could finally hold.

A purpose he could finally feel pulsing inside his ribs.

His pain was not random.

His delays were not punishments.

His losses were not failures.

His heartbreaks were not endings.

His detours were not mistakes.

They were messages — from a universe that speaks in its own language.

And today, he understood that language.

He stood with a heart stitched back together, not perfectly, but beautifully.

He stood with a mind quieter than ever and stronger than ever.

He stood with a soul that no longer begged for direction; it *became* the direction.

He was no longer the boy who doubted himself, no longer the man who carried wounds like weight, no longer the soul that felt lost in a world moving too fast. He was something new.

Someone whole, Someone earned.

He spoke again—this time not a whisper, but a declaration, a promise, a cosmic truth:

"I am ready for life.

And life — I am ready for everything you have been holding for me."

It was not arrogance.

It was not hope.

It was acceptance.

Acceptance that he was worthy.

Acceptance that he was capable.

Acceptance that he was enough, not because the world said so, but because he had finally said so to himself.

He lifted his face to the sky and let the universe hear him, feel him, witness him:

"Thank you for every road that broke me.

Thank you for every road that built me.

Thank you for every road that raised me."

This was not a goodbye to the past.

This was a salute to the future.

A promise that from this moment forward:

He would walk with courage.

He would choose peace over noise.

He would trust timing over fear.

He would love without holding back.

He would forgive without hesitation.

He would live without shrinking his soul.

He would let go of everything that dimmed his light.

And he would keep becoming endlessly, fearlessly, beautifully. Because the man who once questioned his place in this world now claimed it.

The man who once whispered to life now announced himself to the universe.

Not as a survivor.

Not as a seeker.

But as a **reborn being** who finally understood:

The universe was not working against him.

It was waiting for him.

And as Ameya stepped into the next chapter of his existence, calm in his chest, fire in his eyes, softness in his heart, he carried one message for every soul who would ever read his story:

Rise.

Begin again.

Become again.

Because the universe listens to the moment you decide to speak your truth.

And on that day, the universe listened. The stars listened. Life listened.

Because a man who has finally met himself speaks with a voice that echoes across existence.

Final Closing Note From The Author

If you have reached this page, it means you walked beside Ameya through every shadow, every doubt, every lesson, every rise.

But this book was never just about him.

It was about *you*.

About the roads you have walked.

About the storms you have survived silently.

About the dreams you have carried quietly inside your chest.

Every reader who picked up this book has lived their own untold story.

I wrote this book for that story

for the version of you that felt lost,

for the version of you that kept going despite fear,

for the version of you that broke but still chose to rise.

Life will not always be kind.

It will test your patience, your will, your faith.

But it will also shape you into someone stronger, softer, wiser, and more real than you ever imagined.

If this book has given you even one moment of reflection,

One moment of peace,

One moment where you paused and said,

"Maybe I can rise again,"

Then it has done its job.

Remember this, not just today but for the rest of your life:

You are allowed to begin again.

You are allowed to choose yourself.

You are allowed to rewrite your story.

You owe no one perfection.

You owe yourself the truth.

The world doesn't need a flawless you—

It needs a *brave* you,

a *healing* for you,

a *becoming* you.

If Ameya's journey touched your heart, let it also ignite something within you—

a belief that you deserve peace,

that you deserve clarity,

that you deserve love,

that you deserve the life you keep imagining.

Carry this book like a reminder:

every road you walk—good or bad—

is leading you somewhere meaningful.

As you close these pages, I leave you with one final message:

May your fears become smaller,

may your courage become louder,

and may you always trust the quiet voice inside you that says—

"This is not the end. I am still becoming."

Thank you for reading.

Thank you for feeling.

Thank you for walking these roads with me.

This is not goodbye.

This is the beginning of your next chapter.

Ten Life Lessons from "The Roads That Raised Me"

1. Your hardest moments are not punishments, they are preparations.

Life delays, redirects, and reshapes you so you can grow into the person you need to become.

2. Letting go is not losing; it is choosing peace over pain.

The things that leave your life often create space for what is meant to arrive.

3. Gratitude is the bridge between chaos and clarity.

The moment you begin appreciating small joys, big storms lose their power.

4. Healing is not a straight road; it is a series of waves.

Some days you'll rise, some days you'll fall. What matters is that you keep moving.

5. Your past does not define you; your response to it does.

Mistakes are not chains; they are lessons that teach you who you are becoming.

6. Positive thinking is not pretending; it is choosing a better direction.

Your thoughts shape your decisions, your decisions shape your path, and your path shapes your life.

7. You cannot control people, only your boundaries.

Not everyone will treat you right, but you always have the power to protect your peace.

8. Love yourself through your imperfect seasons.

You were trying your best even when you didn't have the clarity you have today.

9. Life's timing is mysterious but meaningful.

You are not late; you are being aligned. What is meant for you will never miss you.

10. You can always begin again.

No matter how scattered your journey has been, you carry the power to restart, rebuild, and rise.

****END****